The Adventures of Obi and Titi

The Hidden Temple of Ogiso

Written by O.T Begho

'The Hidden Temple of Ogiso'

Published in Great Britain by
Evolution Media Lab Ltd

First Printing: 2014

ISBN: 978-0-9554966-1-5

www.obiandtiti.com

Note to readers

At the end of this book, you will find a list of words and their definitions. You can also find these words, quizzes and more on our website at www.obiandtiti.com.

<u>Prologue</u>

Thousands of years ago, long before westerners had visited the shores of Africa, there reigned a great kingdom called Benin. This kingdom was ruled by a great and wise Oba (King), called Oba Eweka.

This story tells of an immense darkness spreading across the Oba's beloved kingdom and the journey of two young children, who find themselves caught in the middle. Only their courage, smart-thinking and a naughty little monkey named Mumu can save them as their decisions change the course of African history forever.

Contents

Chapter 1
Hide and Seek - 11

Chapter 2
The Hidden Temple of Ogiso - 23

Chapter 3
Catch Me If You Can - 33

Chapter 4
Mumu the Naughty Monkey - 45

Chapter 5
The Chamber of Knowledge - 59

Chapter 6
No Way Out − 73

Chapter 7
The Map of Stars − 85

Chapter 8
The Uninvited − 95

The End

Vocabulary − 111

African Facts − 117

Chapter 1

Hide and Seek

Deep in the heart of the Benin kingdom, in an ancient city hidden far, far away, there lived a boy called Obi and a girl named Titi. Obi was nine years old and was always getting into trouble. Fortunately for him, Titi was always close by to help bail him out.

Titi was eleven and was the Oba's only daughter. And because of the close friendship between their fathers, Obi and Titi had become like brother and sister.

Obi's father, Joromi, was the Oba's greatest warrior. Songs of his bravery were sung throughout the land as his skill and strength were unmatched.

Some say Joromi, bored of fighting mere mortals, frequently travelled into the afterworld to battle with beasts and demons and was always victorious.

Sadly, many years ago, Obi's father had set off on a long, dangerous journey and never returned. It was said that the Oba had sent him to search for the hidden temple of Ogiso, but until this very day nobody had seen or heard from him. Some say he still searches the land for the mysterious temple, while others say the beasts and demons from the afterworld came back to reclaim his soul.

Many years had passed since he had left and Obi had grown up in the house of the Oba as Obi's own mother had died during his birth. The Oba treated Obi like his own son and Obi and Titi had been brought up to love one another like family, even though they fought nearly every day.

One day, Obi and Titi were in the forest playing hide and seek. It was Obi's turn to hide and he planned to find the best hiding place ever. Once Titi's eyes were closed and she had started counting, Obi ran as fast as he could down a narrow overgrown path. He quickly looked around. If he continued to follow the path it would lead him further into the forbidden forest. To his left was the Ikpoba River, which they had also been warned not to venture near. Which way should he go?

Obi left the path and headed towards the river as fast as he could. He had to get out of sight before Titi saw him. Once he had reached the river bank it started to dawn on him that perhaps this was not one of his brightest ideas. The bushes were too small to hide behind and the trees were too big to climb. The only place he could see to hide was in the river itself. *Well, that was as good a place as any* he thought. In fact, Titi would never think to look there.

Obi slowly waded out into the water looking for what might be a shallow area to crouch down in. The water was freezing cold, but it was too late to turn back now as he was sure Titi had already started looking for him.

He had reached about a quarter of the way out and was just about to stop when something yanked hard on his leg. He looked down to see what it was, but before he knew it he was underwater struggling to catch his breath. Whatever it was, was dragging him down and fast. He kicked and twisted trying to pull himself free, but it was useless. It was then he remembered what his father used to say. *'Never panic. Use your head not your heart.'*

Obi reached down and felt for what was coiled around his leg. It felt like a thick rope, but smooth and slippery, that was when he saw a head and yellow piercing eyes staring straight at him.

He tried hard to loosen the coil, but it just

seemed to get tighter and tighter as it dragged him along the river bed. As he looked down he could just make out what looked like a broken crocodile's tooth sticking out of the mud; without thinking he grabbed it and aimed straight at the creature's eye.

He could not be sure if he had hit it, but it loosened its grip. He swung at it again, this time directly at the coil around his leg and just as he was about to do it a third time the creature struck out with its razor sharp teeth.

Obi only had a split second to move and as he did so he slammed the crocodile's tooth down as hard as he could on the creature's head.

The coil around Obi's leg loosened. This was his chance. He grabbed it and pulled it off, then started swimming towards the surface faster than he had ever swum before. When he finally broke the surface he gasped for air frantically. He needed to get to the river bank and fast. Unfortunately, this was going to be easier said than done.

The Ikpoba River was well known for its strong currents, which they say is caused by Mammy Waters (Mermaids) dancing on the river bed, praying for fishermen to fall in. Right now, the current was dragging him straight to its centre and he knew he didn't have much time.

Up ahead Obi could see the river narrowing and there were more trees and weeds there, which he might be able to hold on to. He had to reach the bank now, time was running out.

He swam harder and harder, not stopping for a second. Ahead, he could see a long branch with its leaves dipping in and out of the water. He stretched out his hand and grabbed it just as he was passing. The river yanked his bottom half and for a split second he thought he was going to be ripped in two. Thankfully, he was able to hold on and with the last piece of energy left in him, he pulled himself out of the water and on to the river bank, just before his arms gave way.

He had made it, but how stupid had he been. All the children had been warned about the river and the creatures that lurked below, but most of them believed that they were just stories. Now, he knew better.

Obi looked around slowly. He hadn't realised until now, but the river ran straight through the heart of the forbidden forest, so those were two rules he had broken today.

He had been dragged so far away from his original spot that he wasn't sure where he was anymore. He needed to find his bearings. He needed to find Titi.

Reluctantly, he began to call out to Titi, hoping she was close enough to hear him. Obi hated losing hide and seek, but that was not important right now, getting out of the forbidden forest was.

Straight ahead of him was a clearing with a big mango tree right at its centre. He could climb it and see where he was. It would not be too hard as he was a good climber. In fact *he was the best climber he knew*, he thought to himself confidently.

He took a short run up and jumped onto the first branch and then onto the second and then the third.

"Champion!" Obi said, praising himself again.

He hadn't realised it, but his feet were still a little wet and as he stretched out his hand to grab the next branch he slipped.

'Pride always comes before a fall,' he remembered Titi saying as he desperately tried to regain his balance, but it was too late.

Obi slowly fell backwards and watched the blue sky and trees go by him as he headed faster and faster towards the ground.

Chapter 2

The Hidden Temple of Ogiso

Obi landed on a pile of leaves and branches, but surprisingly this didn't help break his fall. Instead, he kept falling straight through the ground into a deep, dark hole. When he finally hit solid ground, it was with a hard, loud thud. The pain shot through his body like a bolt of lightning and then everything went black.

When Obi finally awoke it was with a throbbing headache and a bruised bottom. He slowly got to his feet, dusted himself off and looked around. At first he could not see much, but after a while his eyes adjusted to the dim light that flittered through the hole from the forest above.

He had landed in a small, musky smelling cave. The walls were soft like clay and came away in his hand and the roots of the trees above twisted in and out. But, something was not quite right. At the furthest end of the cave there were no roots and the walls were smooth. And as he looked more closely he couldn't believe what was lying in front of him.

Just as he was about to move forward to examine it he heard an all too familiar voice.

"Oh, you are in big trouble," Titi shouted down at him. "What kind of silly hiding place is this and you do know you are not allowed to enter the forbidden forest. Which part of FORBIDDEN don't you understand!" She added sarcastically.

"I think you should come down and see this," Obi said, ignoring her and before she could say anything else he had disappeared from view.

Obi had moved closer to the object to get

a better look. It was so out of place here in this deep, dark hole. How had it got here?

"What is that?" Titi asked, after carefully climbing down.

"It's my Father's spear," Obi said quietly as if someone else might hear.

"How do you know that?"

"See those white feathers tied to the end," Obi said, pointing. "I gave them to him."

Obi went to pick up the spear, but as he did so Titi stopped him.

"I think this is the hidden temple of Ogiso," she said, excitedly. "The one they used to tell us about when we were younger."

"Centuries ago it was said that a great temple was built in the centre of the kingdom and in it were treasures beyond imagination," Titi said, smugly. "They say..."

"Okay, okay. Why do you think this is it?" Obi interrupted quickly as he could sense that this was leading up to one of her long boring stories.

"Because of that!" Titi said, pointing knowingly.

Right above where the spear was rested was a strange symbol carved into the rock. Obi turned and looked. She was right. He had seen older children draw that shape in the sand hundreds of times as they pretended they were going to look for treasure.

He leaned forward and examined the symbol more closely and then looked at the spear.

"And this isn't a wall," he smiled proudly. "It's a door! Look, some of the feathers are stuck underneath."

Titi moved in for a closer look and saw that he was right. She took the spear, pushed it under the rock and both of them heaved. At first it didn't move, but after a few more pushes the stone door started to move upwards.

Obi and Titi slipped underneath, the light

from the hole barely illuminated what seemed to look like a long stone passageway.

Just as their eyes were getting used to the dark, the spear cracked and the door came down with a loud bang. Now it was really dark and all they could see were each other's eyes and then someone else's.

Whoever or whatever it was blinked twice, gave a yelp and ran fast in the opposite direction. Obi grabbed Titi's arm and started running after it, skilfully following the sound of its footsteps. Titi felt herself being pulled left, then right then left again and just managed to stop herself from falling as they entered a very small room.

The room was dimly lit by a fire burning quietly away in the middle. It cast scary shadows on the wall all around them. Obi quickly looked around to see if what, or who, they had followed into the room was hiding. Titi stayed quietly behind him.

"I don't think anyone else is here," Titi said, breaking the silence.

"Whoever it was must have gone through there," she added pointing to a passage on the right.

"Or *whatever* it was might have gone through there," Obi said, pointing to a passage on the left.

"Let's go through here," Obi said, looking towards the larger left passage.

"Who gave you the right to be leader?"

"Oh, nobody," Obi said, smiling. "You can stay here if you like."

He knew she was still scared and wasn't going to stay there by herself. He was still in charge for now.

Obi went to the middle of the room and carefully picked up one of the burning sticks and headed towards the left passage, with Titi following closely behind him.

Chapter 3

Catch Me If You Can

As they entered the passage, the light from the stick lit up their surroundings. It looked very grimy. After walking a few yards Obi noticed some old torches sticking out of the walls, but before he could make a decision on whether to light one or not Titi grabbed the stick out of his hand and held the flame up against one of the torches. It lit up immediately, but to their astonishment so did all the others.

"Hey, what did you do that for?" Obi shouted, still trying to decide whether it was a good idea or not.

"Shhh! I heard something, this way," Titi said, pushing past him as she headed down the passage.

She was sure she had heard a noise, but was a bit confused as a few yards ahead of her was a solid stone wall. "So where is it you are going?!" Obi said sarcastically, looking over her shoulder.

Ignoring him, she moved closer to the wall. There was something faintly written on it. *"To see me properly I'll give you more light, but this generous gift might soon end your plight. If you get the answer correct I will go away, but if you get it wrong a dear price you will pay!"*

Obi and Titi both looked at each other. What did it mean? Suddenly, they heard a loud crackling sound behind them. They both turned around to see the burning torches spitting out flames wildly across the passage and heading slowly towards them. Their path was now completely blocked and it was getting very, very hot.

"I told you not to light it! Look what you've done," Obi said, sounding less sarcastic and more worried this time.

"Stop complaining and help me solve the riddle," Titi said, turning back towards the wall.

With more light she could see that there was something else written underneath.

"Give it to me and I'll live. Take it away and I'll die!"

Immediately underneath these inscriptions was a small stone head with fire like hair and its mouth wide open.

Does this thing want some food? *Well, even if it did, they didn't have any with them*, Obi thought to himself. It all sounded like gibberish to him and from what he could see they didn't have much time.

"Any ideas?" Obi asked hopefully.

By this time Titi had moved closer to the wall and was examining it more carefully.

"I think I've got it. Come here and give me your hand," Titi said, excitedly.

As Obi stepped forward, she took his hand and pushed it towards the small stone head's mouth. Obi quickly yanked it away.

"Are you crazy?! If you want to give it a hand to eat then let it have your own. I like having two hands."

"No, stupid! Look. Put your hand here,

there is hot air blowing from its mouth," she said, putting her hand near it to show that nothing bad would happen.

Obi took a closer look then reluctantly stretched out his hand towards the front of the stone head. She was right, he could feel the warm air blowing through it.

"Quickly, we have to block it. What have you got on you?" Titi asked.

With a slightly puzzled look on his face Obi put his hands in his pockets and started to pull out their contents. From his right pocket he pulled out a small green, flat looking stone, which was one of his prized possessions, a catapult, which he used for hunting small prey and a decaying lizard's head, one of his unfortunate victims.

From his other pocket he pulled out some wet groundnuts and a small dirty cloth, which he used to protect his head from the sun.

"Yuck, why do you keep that thing? Titi said, looking at the lizard's head. "Oh, that will do," she said, grabbing the cloth.

She scrunched it up and shoved it straight into the stone head's mouth and as if by magic the fire behind them started to move back and simmer down.

"How did you know that that would

work? " asked Obi trying not to show his utter relief.

"Mama is always making me blow air into the fire when she is cooking. Fire needs air to survive. Cut it off and it dies. You would have known that if you ever came to the kitchen before the food was ready!"

Obi was trying to think of a sarcastic reply, but before he could, a loud grinding sound started coming from behind the wall. Slowly, the wall with the writing and small stone head started to move backwards until it revealed another passage hidden behind it.

Obi raised up the torch to see further

down the passage. This time they did not have to follow any sound as they could make out a shadow disappearing at the other end. By the time they had reached it, they were both panting for air. In front of them was a short staircase with a few steps leading downwards.

"Hey, how do we know this isn't a trap?" Titi said, still panting and holding on to Obi to slow him down.

"We don't," Obi said, not giving it a second thought, as he headed down the steps, but as he did so the floor suddenly disappeared from underneath him.

This time, luckily for him, Titi was right

behind him holding his arm tightly. She quickly leant to one side and just managed to swing Obi towards the opposite ledge before losing her grip. Obi grabbed the other side and flipped himself back up onto the landing opposite her.

"Thanks," he said, looking down into the hole.

This was the second time that had happened to him today. Was she right, could this be a trap?

Obi stretched his hand out to Titi, but she just laughed and took a few steps back, ran, jumped, hit the side of the wall with both feet, somersaulted in mid-air and landed softly beside him.

"Show off," Obi said, but just as Titi was going to reply she noticed the shadow they had been chasing, hovering right behind them.

This time it was not running away, it was right around the corner and heading towards them. Now, it looked bigger and more menacing than ever.

It was too late to turn back; they would not be able to make the jump over the gaping hole without a good run up.

Obi still had the stick, but the fire was out. He held it up in front of him. They looked at each other and without saying a word both charged round the corner and into a small room screaming.

They stopped dead in their tracks. They could never have imagined what was round the corner waiting for them.

Chapter 4

Mumu the Naughty Monkey

Standing right there, in front of them, was a little monkey with big round eyes and a smile nearly twice the size of its head. What was even more shocking was that they knew exactly who this monkey was. His name was Mumu.

A few years ago, a day before Obi's 5th birthday, Obi's father had brought Mumu home as a birthday present, but on the morning of his birthday Mumu was seen running off with all of Obi's birthday gifts. A few days later he was caught and brought back to the house, but Obi's presents were nowhere to be found.

Obi was very angry and wished they hadn't found Mumu as he was a continuous nuisance and could not be trusted to keep his hands off anything. Unfortunately, Obi's father saw the funny side to this and made Obi keep him.

To Obi's great relief, however, one day someone left Mumu's cage door wide open and he was never seen again, until now.

"I don't believe this, what is he doing here?" Obi said, looking over suspiciously at Mumu, but before Titi could answer they both got an even bigger shock.

"Obi, Titi my friends. Welcome, oh. Long time," Mumu said, still grinning from ear to ear.

Obi and Titi looked at each other in disbelief. Since when do monkeys talk?

They stood there for a second looking at Mumu, not sure if it had really happened. Obi moved closer and said quietly "Did you just say something?"

"Yes, oh!" Mumu said cheerfully, making them both jump backwards.

"I said, 'Long time.' How you *dey*?"

This time there was no mistaking it, Mumu had actually spoken English, or was that Pidgin English?

After the initial shock had worn off, they started asking him a hundred and one questions, all at once.

"Slow down please, you *dey* talk too fast," Mumu replied.

"Ok," said Obi, moving closer, "When you saw us why did you run away and why were you trying to kill us?"

"I wasn't trying to kill you, oh. Mumu would never do such a *ting*," he said, with an exaggerated look of shock on his face.

"I have fallen down that very hole many times before," he added as he pointed to several bumps on his head.

Obi remembered how sneaky Mumu could be. Now if Mumu could talk it also meant he could lie and that was not good.

"So how come you can talk?" Obi asked suspiciously.

Mumu smiled proudly. "I drank from the fountain of healing and knowledge," he said, pointing to what looked like a rusty old tap, dripping in the corner of the room.

Obi and Titi thought he must be joking,

but the look on his face was very serious.

"After drinking I could talk and sing oh, would you like me to sing for you?" he asked them eagerly.

To Mumu's great disappointment, Obi said "No!"

Titi could see Mumu was upset so she moved forward and asked in a nice friendly voice, "So, how did you get here?"

"Oh, that's a funny story," he said, warming up again.

"One day, I *dey* forest eating pawpaw and bananas when I *see* Obi's papa. It looked like he was looking for something so, of course, I followed him.

"He wandered further and further into the forest until he came to the tree, the one right outside the entrance. I saw him climb into the cave and he did not come out for two days.

"Anyway, after that I didn't see him again, oh. Then one day as I *dey* sit in my tree eating..."

"Yes, we know, eating pawpaw and bananas. Get on with the story," urged Obi irritably.

"Well," continued Mumu. "I saw your papa heading back towards the cave again. He looked like he was injured so this time when he went in the cave, of course, I followed him and I was able to slip underneath the door just before it closed.

"I followed him for hours and hours and I was so hungry, because I had not finished eating my..." he stopped quickly thinking better of mentioning his favourite food again.

"Well, I found him in here on the floor, oh! He must have known I had been following him because he was not surprised to see me. In fact, he asked if I had gotten lost."

Obi laughed quietly to himself. His father used to say that to him all the time when they went hunting. It was so hard for anyone to keep up with his father.

"He was injured quite badly," said Mumu continuing, "but he was more worried about the map."

"The map, what map?" asked Obi and Titi eagerly.

"He said we had to find the map, the Map of Stars. It would show him where everything was. I thought, *he don craze*," said Mumu, demonstrating what he thought crazy looked like.

"He was very weak so I gave him some of that water and suddenly his skin began to glow and his wounds started to heal by themselves," said Mumu reliving the moment in his head.

"Then as I was going to help him up he stopped me and started laughing. He said he now knew the location of the map."

"Was it the magic water that had showed him?" Titi immediately asked.

"Oh, no," replied Mumu pointing up. "It was the ceiling."

Obi and Titi slowly looked up at the high ceiling and under the faint light they could just make out a faded picture. It was a drawing of the Temple of Ogiso showing all its corridors and rooms and right in the middle was a room labelled *Chamber of Knowledge*.

"So," Mumu said, trying to get their

attention back, "he memorised the path to the Chamber of Knowledge and we made our way there. Unfortunately, we got lost many, many times. When we got back here your papa found some paper and ink and copied the map and then my dear friend, your papa, left!"

"That seems a bit strange," Titi said, slowly looking over at Obi and then back at Mumu. "Why did he leave you here?"

"Obi's papa wanted me to stay here and guard the place," Mumu answered puffing out his chest, but giving up after a couple of seconds as it hurt him too much.

Obi didn't believe a word of it. Why

would his father leave Mumu here? The place was falling to pieces and there didn't seem to be anything of value that they could see.

It was Titi who accidentally stumbled on the answer. While they were standing in the room talking she had noticed something shiny sticking out of a bag in the corner of the room. She headed over to it and lifted it up. There was something very heavy inside.

"That's not mine, oh," Mumu shouted before Titi had even opened it, but when she did, out poured gold coins, diamonds and trinkets. They both looked over at Mumu.

"It's not mine, oh" he said again a bit

more quietly this time, but the pawpaw and bananas sitting in the midst of the pile of gold told another story.

"That's why my father left you in here. He caught you trying to steal," Obi said, holding the stick up in front of him.

For a moment it looked like Mumu was bowing his head down in shame, but as Obi looked closer he saw that Mumu was actually eyeing up a coin that had rolled next to his foot.

"So where is the map and think twice before you lie again," Obi said, poking Mumu's fat belly and trying to get his attention back.

"Your papa put it back" said Mumu, still

looking down.

"Where?"

"Come. I will show you," replied Mumu raising his head cheerfully.

Within seconds Mumu had repacked his loot and started heading out of the room.

"Wait. I think we should take our time to memorise the directions on the ceiling properly. We don't want to get lost," Titi said wisely and they all nodded in agreement.

Chapter 5

The Chamber of Knowledge

After a few wrong turns and even more arguments, the three of them finally reached the doors of the Chamber of Knowledge. Now, they could easily see why Obi's father had put the map back here and not worried about Mumu getting his little hands on it.

The doors were ten times their size and there was an enormous piece of wood slid between its iron handles. It would have been impossible for Mumu to move it and might even be for Obi and Titi.

Just as Titi moved towards the door, Obi stopped her.

"Shhh, I think I heard something," he said putting his finger to his lips.

"What is it?"

"It's my *belle*!" Mumu said shyly, rubbing his pot belly.

"Come on let's get the wood off," said Titi, walking past them and over to the door.

She tried pushing it but it didn't move.

"So my father knew I would come?" Obi asked Mumu, while joining in on Titi's efforts.

"Yes," Mumu said, without moving a step to help them.

"But I don't think he expected you to come so soon. You are still very small and he said the journey ahead is very dangerous. Why don't we all come back later?"

Both of them gave Mumu a very stern look, which made him think twice about saying anything else. They turned back and tried the door again.

It took them nearly ten minutes and all of

their strength to finally get the wood to budge.

When the doors opened they stood back in awe. The room was gigantic, rows of cabinets full of books lined the walls from the floor to the ceiling. They contained hundreds, if not thousands, of years of African history. Obi and Titi looked at each other.

"This is going to be slightly harder than we thought," Obi said.

Titi nodded quietly in agreement.

At this point Mumu dropped his bag, strolled straight past them, climbed on one of the cabinets and pulled out a map from amongst dozens of others.

"Here it is," he said cheerfully, without batting an eyelid.

"How do you know that's it?" Obi asked, not convinced.

"Oh, this was where we found it the first time and see, it has the mark."

Sure enough on the outside of the map you could clearly see a yellow looking star right above a temple. It was the hidden Temple of Ogiso. Obi laughed to himself. His father always used to tell him to put things back exactly where he found them, this time he could really see why that was good advice.

They laid it down on the table in the

middle of the room and rolled it open. Their eyes widened as they slowly took in every detail. It was like no map they had ever seen before. It was alive, the oceans moved, the desert sands swirled. They could even hear the sound of the wind, it was magnificent.

"Okay, now you have seen it oh, can we go?" asked Mumu, seemingly not interested.

Before either of them could answer they heard a loud growling sound coming from the shadows outside the room. As they looked down the corridor they could see a huge wolf-like creature running towards them. It was already half-way down the corridor before they had even breathed.

"Quick, get the door," Titi shouted running towards the doors.

Obi was by her side in seconds. They pulled the doors and slammed them shut. Titi grabbed the inner door latch and pulled it down just in time. CRASH! Whatever it was had smashed right into the door and the impact threw Obi and Titi flat across the floor.

Neither of them got up. They both stayed there watching the door quietly, too scared to make a sound or even move. Then they heard a loud growl, which sent a shiver down their spines and then another crash. The door wouldn't last long under this kind of battering.

Mumu was the one that finally broke the silence.

"I told you we should have come back later. Obi you have not changed at all, always getting us into trouble. Titi, *I beg*. Please let us find a place to hide."

"I have an even better idea," said Titi, getting up quickly, "let's get out of here."

She grabbed the map, rolled it up and started heading to the other end of the chamber.

"Where are you going?" Obi asked catching up with her.

"I remember seeing another entrance into

this room on the map," she said, without slowing down, "and it was right here."

She had stopped in front of a tall shelf full of dusty old maps.

"Well, that clearly isn't a door," said Obi, stating the obvious.

At this point Mumu began shrieking hysterically, waving his hands in the air and swinging his tail. Obi was just about to give him a hard knock on his head, partly to shut him up, but more so for his cheeky comments. That was when they all saw it.

During Mumu's hysteria he had accidentally knocked some books and maps off the shelf and through the gap they could see a small passageway. Mumu had actually been helpful for once.

"Come on help me move the cabinet," Obi shouted.

"We don't have time for that," Titi said, flinging the maps and books to the floor. "We'll have to squeeze through."

There was a loud crack and then a crashing sound as the doors to the chamber finally gave way.

"Quick, let's go," Obi whispered.

Titi went through first and just as Obi was about to climb through he stopped and turned to Mumu.

"Mumu, quickly climb up and get one of the fire sticks."

Mumu looked back petrified.

"I'm not climbing up there, I want to go through the hole with Titi."

"Do it now or I'll leave you here with that thing," Obi said, angrily.

Mumu didn't like the sound of that and could see arguing wouldn't get him anywhere, so reluctantly he dropped his loot and started to climb.

The room was silent now except for the slight creaking of the shelf as Mumu made his way up. He had just gotten the fire stick in his hand and was climbing down when he saw the beast hurtling down the middle aisle. Unfortunately, it had seen him too.

Mumu yelped, dropped the torch and flew straight past Obi and into the hole. As Obi knelt down to retrieve the torch he could hear the creature coming round the corner, but instead of jumping through the hole he started picking up maps.

"Obi what are you doing?" Titi screamed.

"Buying us some time," he yelled back as he finally jumped through the hole.

He could smell the beast's foul breath

right behind him. Without looking up he dropped the maps in front of the hole and held out the torch above them. Just as he was about to light them the creature took a swipe at him with its large, razor sharp claws. Luckily, Obi was just out of reach, but it had hit the fire stick out of his hand. The stick bounced off the wall, hit the ground and slowly rolled to where the pile of maps were. The maps were so dry that they burst into flames immediately catching the creature's claw, which was directly above it. The wolf-like creature gave off a loud hideous howl and backed off.

"Let's get out of here," Obi said, picking

up the stick, visibly shaking.

This time there were no complaints.

Chapter 6

No Way Out

Unlike other parts of the temple, this section smelt damp and moist and the further they went the stronger the smell became.

Obi saw a torch up ahead and used his fire to light it. Once again all the torches in the corridor magically lit up, but thankfully nothing else happened this time.

Now they could see why it smelt so bad. The walls and floor were all wet and had algae and moss growing on them. The further they went down the corridor the wetter it became. As they turned the next corner they were faced with steep steps leading down. Unfortunately, these led straight into a big pool of water.

They all stopped and looked at each other. There was no way of telling how deep it was. Mumu had been quiet up until this point, but he had gotten over his shock.

"Oh, this foolish boy has chosen the wrong way," he said, looking at Obi whilst standing well behind Titi in case of any repercussions.

Obi didn't say a word, but quietly wondered to himself if monkeys could swim as well as they could climb trees.

He turned towards the steps, this time he would be more careful. He slowly took the first one, then the second and third. By this time the water was all the way up to his knees.

"It's okay," he said, moving forward more quickly. "No more steps..." Then suddenly without warning he disappeared from view.

Titi screamed, but quickly covered her mouth. Not again. She about to jump in when Obi popped up laughing.

"Argh," Titi scowled. "This is not the time for your childish games."

Obi smiled.

"I wasn't playing, there is a hole down here, but it's okay this time, it's our way out. See," he said, pointing and sure enough Titi could see a dim fluttering of light. It looked like daylight.

"Come on," Obi said.

"What about the map?" Titi asked.

Obi looked at her.

"We don't really have a choice. We can't leave it, we'll dry it when we get out."

"What about Mumu?" Mumu asked, looking at the water quite scared.

Obi still felt that Mumu was not to be trusted, probably another one of the reasons his father left him in here.

"We can't leave him here, he did help us find the map," said Titi as if reading Obi's mind.

Obi was very reluctant, but stretched out his hand and pulled Mumu onto his back.

All three of them took a deep breath as they went underwater. Within a few seconds they could see the light and quickly headed towards it. Obi was first out with Mumu holding on to his neck for dear life and nearly strangling him.

"Where are we?" Titi asked, catching her breath after breaking the surface.

"We are in a well," Obi replied, trying to pull Mumu off and still stay afloat.

Titi looked up and wondered whether this was actually a good idea, it was a long way up, but going back wasn't an option.

"Come on, you first," Obi said as he tugged on the rope and bucket and pushed it towards her.

Titi grabbed the rope and started to pull herself up. Mumu jumped off Obi's shoulder and quickly followed her. Obi took one last look into the water and then slowly pulled himself up after them. This was the last time he would disobey his elders he promised himself.

When he got to the top he found Titi looking at the map with a very puzzled look on her face.

"What's wrong?" he asked.

"Nothing," she said. "Look, it's completely dry."

Obi looked at the map. It was like nothing had ever happened. It looked just the same as when they first opened it.

"We better get going," Titi said, folding it up again.

Obi stood up to leave and it was only then that he noticed Mumu's absence.

"Oh, no! Where did he go?" Obi asked Titi.

Titi shrugged her shoulders.

Then from nowhere, something hit Obi square between his eyes.

"Ouch!"

"Hey, foolish boy. I was going to be rich. I could have been the king of the monkeys," Mumu shouted from a nearby tree.

Obi started to head towards Mumu, but Titi blocked his path.

"We can't let him go," Obi said, trying to push by her "that's why my father left him in there, he'll tell everyone!"

"Somehow I don't think that's going to happen," said Titi, reassuringly. "He is way too greedy to do that. Come on, leave him. Let's go home."

Obi thought about it for a second and realised she was probably right, and it was getting dark. They both turned and started heading in the direction of what they believed was the city.

"Oh, look who is running away now! If it wasn't for me you would have been dinner for our creature friend back there," shouted Mumu as he tried pelting Obi with another rock, but by this time Obi and Titi were out of reach and could barely hear him.

They continued on the path for a while and came to an area that looked familiar. They were right at the edge of the forest and they could just make out the rooftops of the houses. After walking for a little while, they arrived outside the side gate of the palace.

"When we get inside, go straight to our room. I'll go and greet Papa and make up some excuse as to why we missed dinner," Titi said as they entered the palace grounds.

"Titi, Obi, both of you get in here right now!" Titi's father shouted, staring straight at them from an upstairs window.

Now, they were really in trouble.

Chapter 7

The Map of Stars

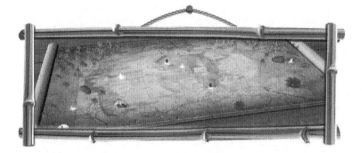

Titi's father had been sitting on the veranda for most of the evening watching the palace gates. He had just gone into his room when he spotted Obi and Titi from his window sneaking in through the side entrance.

He was very angry and unluckily for them, Titi's mother had travelled to see her father in Sapele, so she would not be there to save them from his wrath today.

"Where have you two been?" he asked looking at them from head to toe. "And why are you wet? Didn't I warn you not to go near the river?" he added as he pulled some weed-like plant out of Titi's wet and tangled hair.

Titi opened her mouth to say something, but thought better of it. Obi just stood there with his head down.

"What is that behind your back?"

The Oba stretched out his hand to take it, but then froze in shock. Clearly marked on the side of the scroll-like object was the unmistakable sign of the hidden temple of Ogiso.

"Where did you get that?" the Oba asked, knowing, fully well, it could have only come from one place.

"You have been in the temple," he said, not waiting for a reply and at this point Obi and Titi offered none. They were more surprised that he knew where they had been.

He took a step back and sat in his chair. He suddenly felt very, very tired.

"We knew someday someone would find it. In fact Obi, your father was sure of it."

Obi wasn't sure what to say so he kept

quiet.

Titi's father continued as though talking to himself.

"We had kept it a secret for many, many years. We were only a little older than yourselves when your father first found it."

Memories of his dear friend came flooding back, he missed Joromi. He beckoned for Titi to bring the map over and after taking it from her he laid it out across the table.

Once the map was opened it immediately came to life. Titi's father looked at it in amazement. He had the same look of surprise that the children had when they first saw it.

Obi and Titi moved slightly closer. They didn't want to upset Titi's father again, so neither of them spoke.

Something was slightly different about the map this time. It had tiny glistening, diamond shaped pieces moving around on it and there were some black ones too.

"Come, sit down, let me tell you a story," said Titi's father.

Surprised, but a little less scared now, they moved closer and sat by his feet.

"They say that many, many centuries ago a great star exploded and that pieces from that star landed here on earth.

"Those pieces of rock, which some called Okutas or Starlights, went unnoticed for hundreds of years. When they were finally discovered it was found that they had mysterious effects on objects as well as the people they came into contact with.

"They say the Okutas could make people do astonishing things, like disappear or transform them into the shape of an animal.

"Some people embedded the Okutas in clothes and other objects and this had even stranger effects," said Titi's father, glancing over at the map.

"There are good people out there who

vowed to keep this secret and only use these powers for good. They have come to be known as Orishas or Guardians. But there are many others whom have been consumed by the power the Okutas wield, and have used them for personal gain and evil. They are known as Ekumeku, the silent ones," he said, in a low voice.

"If I am right and the stories are true about this map, then these sparkling stones," he said, pointing to the map and moving pieces, "show the location of Okutas or objects and the black ones, which were once pure and bright are now in the hands of Ekumeku."

All three of them leaned over the map to take a closer look. Just as Obi was about to say something a loud bell went off outside. There was shouting, and then a few minutes later a knock on the door. Titi's father quickly folded up the map and placed it inside his desk drawer.

"Come in," he said.

"Oba, sir, there are men from the council downstairs, they say they are waiting for you in the town hall," the messenger said, hastily.

"Tell them I am busy," the Oba said, waving him out.

"Oba, sir, the elders said that you should come with them now, right now sir."

The Oba glared at the messenger angrily. This time he was wise enough to leave without saying any more. As he closed the door Titi's father turned to the children.

"I have to go now. We will talk more tomorrow," he said, ushering them out.

They left the room, not daring to ask for the map and headed straight to the kitchen. They had lots to talk about and were very surprised at the story Titi's father had told them, but more than that, they were hungry.

Chapter 8

The Uninvited

Once the children had left, Titi's father took a key from his shelf and locked the map in his drawer. There was no time to look at it now. He had to deal with the matter at hand, the council.

The Oba set off towards the centre of the city with the messenger following closely behind. His thoughts wondered back to the map and his old and dearest friend. Where was he, and was he still alive?

His thoughts were disturbed abruptly as he approached the hall. He could hear raised voices and banging.

"All arise for Oba Eweka," the council's spokesperson announced as Titi's father entered the hall. Everyone stopped talking immediately and rose from their seats.

The Oba took his seat then beckoned for them to all sit down. The hall was nearly full. All the leaders from the six provinces were present.

"Who has ordered this meeting and under

whose authority?" The Oba asked, looking around slowly.

A man rose graciously from the other side of the table wearing a dark long cloak. It had a hood, which covered the wearer's face, but his voice was unmistakable. It was Ezomo the son of late Chief Koko.

"All hail Oba Eweka," Ezomo began, bowing slightly. "It is on a matter of great importance that I have asked the great leaders to all come here tonight."

"But why? You know you no longer have a seat in any of this council's proceedings and your actions in the past have shown that you are not to be trusted."

A few years ago Ezomo had used a gang of mercenaries to forcefully take money from the surrounding villages, pretending to offer them protection. When his father found out, he was so angry that he banished him from their clan. The next day, his father was found dead in his room.

There was no proof that Ezomo had done it, but he never seemed remorseful or repentant and immediately after forcefully took over his father's chieftaincy.

"Yes I know I have not always been helpful, but as a responsible citizen in any community I feel it is my right, in fact, my duty to warn our people of any imminent danger."

A few of the leaders around the table nodded their heads encouragingly and whispers started from the people at the back of the hall.

Oba Eweka could see that Ezomo had been building alliances with other village members. This was not good.

The Oba leaned back in his chair and ushered Ezomo to continue. He knew that he had to play this very carefully so as not to fall into Ezomo's hands.

"It has come to my knowledge that dark forces are moving across the land and they are on their way to our region."

The whispers in the background started getting louder.

"I hear they are in search of something and will stop at nothing to get it. That something is here in this city."

"Nonsense," the Oba retorted. "There has always been evil moving across the region, but up till today it has never come.

"Is this the rubbish you have come to feed the council and scare our people with? Lies, all lies!

"Your father was a dear friend of mine and he would be very disappointed in you."

"My father was weak and he believed your lies like everybody else, but I have seen the truth," Ezomo shouted angrily.

"Listen to me all of you good people," Ezomo said, turning to the crowd. "The Oba has been keeping a secret from you. He knows where the Temple of Ogiso is and has known for many years."

The noise in the hall was now deafening.

"He has been keeping it a secret so he can keep the treasure for himself."

The Oba tried to hide the look of shock on his face, but unfortunately Ezomo had seen it and was now smiling treacherously from under his hood.

The hall had gone quiet again and everyone was waiting for the Oba to say something. He chose his words very carefully.

"Many of you here have been my friends since we were children, and our own children have grown up as friends. Have you ever seen diamonds or gold on my wrist?

"Many of you here have been to my house, have you ever once seen any of such things there. Oh yes, my wife is a diamond, but she is not from the temple."

Many of the elders laughed. They all knew the Oba's wife and she was truly a diamond, but no, she was definitely not from the temple.

"A great danger is coming to our city?" The Oba asked sarcastically.

"Sadly, I fear the great danger is already here," he added looking directly at Ezomo.

"We have all heard stories of your great travels and conquests Ezomo and also about those you share your company with.

"I dearly pray that you have not become a messenger of destruction without even knowing it. This meeting is over!" said the Oba, standing up.

"Oba Eweka has spoken. All hail Oba Eweka," shouted the council spokesperson.

Ezomo tried to protest, but his voice was drowned out by the crowd. The Oba quickly left the hall.

He had a lot to think about and a lot to do, but very little time. One thing he knew was that he must act swiftly or they would all be in grave danger. He hurried back to the house.

"Obi, Titi, wake up," Titi's father whispered, as he entered their room. "There is something you must do." Obi and Titi slowly got up, wiped the sleep from their eyes and listened intently.

"Many things have happened today, which I cannot fully explain; you children finding the map, our uninvited visitor."

The children looked at him confused.

He continued. "This might not all make sense now but today is only part of a much bigger story.

"You see, the temple has protected our kingdom for centuries, but a couple of years ago your father said he had felt the power surrounding it and our city was growing weak.

"I guess I didn't want to believe him because I didn't want him to go. But one day he came to me and said he had to leave to find the other Okutas, so as to protect you Obi, so as to protect all of us."

The children were listening very carefully now. The Oba pulled out the map and a small envelope from his gown.

"Both of you need to leave the city at first light. It is not safe for you here anymore," he said, sullenly.

"You must go to Sapele and give this letter to your mother," he said, handing Titi the envelope. "She will know what to do."

Titi's father handed Obi the map.

"My son, you must guard this with your life just as your father did for so many years and when the time is right you will know what to do."

"I have packed some provisions for you," he said, pointing to two bags by the door.

"They should be enough to last the journey. But that's enough for now. Go to sleep," he said as he headed towards the door.

"You have a long day ahead of you."

Obi and Titi were tired, but found it very hard to fall asleep. They kept going over what had happened to them during the day and what might have happened at the meeting to worry the Oba so much.

They finally drifted off to sleep, but before they knew it cockerels had started crowing and it was time to get up.

"Come on Obi, wake up, we have to go," Titi said, shaking him roughly.

Obi hated waking up in the morning, but today was different. They had a very important mission.

Obi and Titi packed some other things in their bags making sure to conceal the map and envelope properly.

Titi thought about going to say bye to her father, but remembered his instructions were to leave immediately. So, they crept downstairs, into the kitchen, and headed out the back door.

The grounds were quiet. It was still too early for anyone to be awake. They passed through the back gate and started walking down the path that would lead them to the main road.

Titi's father watched them from his bedroom window. They were so young, yet very brave. This would be a dangerous journey, but it would be even more dangerous if they stayed.

There was still a lot they didn't know, but now was not the time to tell them. He had a lot to do if his plan was to work, it must work for all of their sakes.

Obi and Titi walked briskly and had made good time. For most of the trek neither of them said anything, but it was Titi who finally broke the silence.

"Are you scared?" she asked nervously.

"No," Obi replied.

"Liar," she said, hitting him playfully. "It's okay to be scared you know."

"I know, but I'm not," he said, wondering if she could hear his heart pounding in his chest.

They had reached the top of the hill just outside the city and both of them turned instinctively to see their home, one last time. Neither of them realised it at this point, but their adventure had only just begun.

The End .....for now!

Vocabulary

Centuries/Century: A century is one hundred years. Centuries are many hundreds of years.

Sentence: It took the people many centuries to build the pyramids.

Plight: A dangerous, difficult or sad situation.

Sentence: The children had no food or shelter and with the rain coming their plight was only going to get worse.

Repercussion: Usually a negative result of an event, statement or action. An example of a repercussion is a teenager being suspended from school for fighting.

Sentence: The repercussion of being caught stealing is going to jail.

Pidgin English: An informal, simplified language that is a based on English. Similar to slang.

Example: Wetin you dey do? (Pidgin English) This means "What are you doing?"

Sentence: The children loved speaking Pidgin English when their parents were not around.

Waded/Wade: Wade means to walk with effort through water or another liquid.

Sentence: Obi and Titi waded through the water and mud to reach the river bank.

Illuminated/Illuminate: Illuminate means to light up.

Sentence: When Obi lit the candle its flame illuminated the dark room.

Astonishment: Great surprise

Sentence: Titi looked at Obi in astonishment as he hit the target again and again.

Sarcastically/Sarcasm: Saying the opposite of what you really mean in order to insult someone, show irritation or to be funny

Sentence: "Yes, I'll help you," he said, sitting down with his arms crossed and not making any attempt to help.

Inscription: Words that are written on or cut into a surface

Sentence: The inscription on the rock was very clear. It said, "Stay out."

Gibberish: Speech that is meaningless or impossible to understand

Sentence: Obi still had food in his mouth, so when he tried to speak all that came out was gibberish.

Unmistakable: Very clear, not able to mistake something for something else.

Sentence: The difference between an apple and an orange is unmistakable.

Provinces: A region within a country.

Sentence: The province was ruled by a good governor.

Remorseful: Sorry or full of regret.

Example: If you feel bad about having stolen something and you wish you had not done it, this is an example of when you are remorseful.

Sentence: The judge hoped the man would be remorseful after serving his sentence.

Imminent: Soon or about to happen.

Sentence: The clouds were dark and they could tell the rain was imminent.

Alliances: A relationship based on similar goals or interests.

Sentence: The two countries formed an alliance to stop the smugglers.

<u>Treacherously/Treacherous</u>: Someone who is dishonest and cannot be trusted, or something that is dangerous, difficult or hazardous.

Sentence: The sea looked treacherous. There was no way they would have survived the journey.

African Facts

1. The Benin Kingdom was a West African state that was formally established in 1440 AD but initially came into being from 900-1200 AD.

2. The Benin Kingdom was situated in the country that is now known as Nigeria.

3. The first kings in the Benin Kingdom were known as Ogisos and then later they were referred to as Obas.

4. The original people and founders of the Benin Kingdom were the Edo people and the first ruler of the Kingdom, was Ogiso Igodo.

5.   Oba Eweka was the Benin Kingdom's first Oba and came into power after the Ogisos rule ended. It is thought that he ruled from 1180 – 1246.